SCARLATTI

AN INTRODUCTION TO HIS KEYBOARD WORKS

EDITED BY MARGERY HALFORD

CONTENTS

K. refers to the numbers assigned to Scarlatti's works by Ralph Kirkpatrick.

L. refers to the numbers assigned by Allesandro Longo.

L.S. refers to the Supplement to the Longo edition.

For further explanation, see page 5.

Second Edition
Copyright © MMI by Alfred Publishing Co., Inc.
Cover art: Landscape with Roman Ruins
by Giovanni Antonio Canaletto (1697–1768)
Accademia, Venice, Italy
Cameraphoto / Art Resource, New York

ISBN 0-7390-2215-6

DOMENICO SCARLATTI

1685–1757

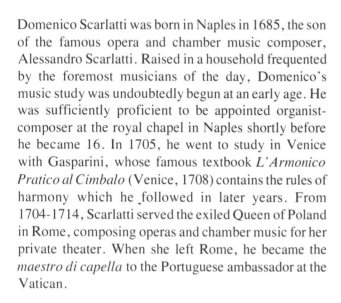

Lithograph by Alfred Lemoine

Domenico Scarlatti was born in Naples in 1685, the son of the famous opera and chamber music composer, Alessandro Scarlatti. Raised in a household frequented by the foremost musicians of the day, Domenico's music study was undoubtedly begun at an early age. He was sufficiently proficient to be appointed organist-composer at the royal chapel in Naples shortly before he became 16. In 1705, he went to study in Venice with Gasparini, whose famous textbook *L'Armonico Pratico al Cimbalo* (Venice, 1708) contains the rules of harmony which he followed in later years. From 1704-1714, Scarlatti served the exiled Queen of Poland in Rome, composing operas and chamber music for her private theater. When she left Rome, he became the *maestro di capella* to the Portuguese ambassador at the Vatican.

While living in Rome, Scarlatti met the foremost musicians of Europe. He and Handel held each other's work in mutual esteem and they engaged in a friendly contest of keyboard abilities. Handel was declared superior at the organ, and Scarlatti at the harpsichord. In his *Memoirs of Handel* (London, 1760), Mainwaring wrote '' . . . the characteristic excellence of Scarlatti seems to have consisted in a certain elegance and delicacy of expression.'' In *A General History of Music* (London, 1789), Charles Burney recounted the story that Thomas Roseingrave told of hearing Scarlatti perform in Rome: ''When he (Scarlatti) began to play, he thought ten hundred d—ls had been at the instrument. He never heard such passages of execution and effect before.'' Roseingrave was so impressed that he followed Scarlatti for some years and after returning to England, published Scarlatti's compositions.

Scarlatti entered the service of King João V at Lisbon in 1720 as chapelmaster and music instructor to the royal children. In 1725, the King's daughter Maria Barbara was betrothed to the Prince of the Asturias and, when they were married in 1729, Scarlatti went to Spain to serve in her court. She became Queen of Spain in 1746 and Scarlatti spent the remainder of his life in her service.

The royal court must have been somewhat gloomy, partly because the King suffered sorely from melancholia, as did Maria Barbara's husband in later years. Farinelli, the most celebrated of all singers, was brought to the court in 1737 and his beautiful singing helped to alleviate the King's depression. Farinelli, too, remained in court service, and although he was never allowed to sing for anyone but the royal family, he produced operas of such excellence and splendor that the Royal Opera of Madrid had no peer in all Europe. The most celebrated musicians of the day were imported for these productions and the musical life of the court must have been stimulating.

During the years in Spain, Scarlatti absorbed the vibrant characteristics of Spanish rhythms and gypsy songs and much of his harpsichord music evokes images of flamenco dancing and the haunting bittersweet Moorish melodies. Burney comments in *The Present State of Music in Germany, the Netherlands and United Provinces* (London, 1775), ''there are many passages in Scarlatti's pieces, in which he imitated the melody of tunes sung by the carriers, muleteers (mule drivers), and common people. He used to say, that the music of Alberti, and of several other modern composers, did not in the execution want a harpsichord, as it might be equally well, or perhaps, better expressed by any other instrument, but, as nature had given him ten fingers, and, as his instrument had employment for them all, he saw no reason why he should not use them.''

Scarlatti wrote some 550 harpsichord sonatas for the Queen, who must have been an excellent performer. King João V knighted him in 1738 and Scarlatti dedicated the set of 30 Sonatas called the *Essercizi* to him. Despite the fact that most of the sonatas were definitely composed for the harpsichord, Scarlatti developed the musical resources of the keyboard so completely and with such ingenuity that he has been called the founder of modern piano technic.

ORIGIN

The present collection contains the easiest works among Scarlatti's more than 550 known sonatas. They were written for his royal pupil and patroness, Queen Maria Barbara of Spain. Since no autographs are known to exist, the primary sources are the manuscript volumes in Venice and Parma and the printed editions published by Roseingrave and Boivin. In the preparation of the present edition, all of the following sources have been consulted:

1. *Sonate Per Cembalo del Cavaliere Dn. Scarlati* (sic). 15 Volumes dated from 1742-1757. Courtesy of the Biblioteca Nationale Marciana, Venice. A facsimile from Volume X is reproduced on page 12 of the present volume.

2. *Scarlatti. Libro 1o* (etc.) 15 Volumes dated from 1742-1757 located in the Biblioteca Palatina, Parma. Facsimile Reprint by Johnson Reprint Corp., New York.

3. Thomas Roseingrave. *XLII Suites de Piéces pour le Clavecin en deux Volumes. Composées par Domenico Scarlatti* (London, 1739). Courtesy of the Library of Congress, Washington, D.C.

4. *Piéces Pour le Clavecin Composées Par Domco. Scarlatti, Maître de Clavecin du Prince des Asturies.* Volume 1; Volume 2. (Paris, no date; ca. 1742). By kind permission of the Provost & Fellows of King's College, Cambridge.

5. Charles Avison. *Twelve Concertos in Seven Parts* (etc.) *done from two books of Lessons for the Harpsichord, composed by Domenico Scarlatti* (London, 1744). Courtesy of the Trustees of the British Museum. A facsimile from this version is reproduced on page 4 of the present volume.

Each of these sources is further described below:

THE VENICE MANUSCRIPTS

These consist of 15 beautifully bound, decorated and illuminated volumes with the combined coats of arms of Spain and Portugal tooled in gold on the covers. They were apparently made for the Queen who bequeathed them to Farinelli, the celebrated singer at her court. We do not know who deposited them in the Biblioteca Marciana in 1835 where they are still located. Each volume measures approximately 24 x 32 cm. They are dated from 1742-1757. The handwriting is clear and legible for the most part, and there appear to be only a few small errors in them. All of the Sonatas in the present collection except K.32, K.34, K.40 and K.42 are contained in the Venice manuscripts as follows: Vol. XIV (1742), K.63, K.73, K.77, K.80, K.81, K.83, K.88, K.89, K.90; Vol. IX (1754), K.391, K.415; Vol. X (1755), K.431, K.440.

THE PARMA MANUSCRIPTS

These consist of another 15 volumes dated from 1742-1757. They are the same size as the Venice manuscripts and the same copyist seems to have written many of them. The Parma volumes are not so beautifully illuminated and bound as the Venice ones. Both sets of manuscript volumes are regarded by scholars as equal in value and authenticity even though there are some small differences between them. The sonatas in the present collection which are in the Parma manuscripts are as follows: Vol. X (1754), K.415; Vol. XI (1754), K.391; Vol. XII (1755), K.431, K.440.

THE ROSEINGRAVE
AND BOIVIN EDITIONS

These editions, which were printed during Scarlatti's lifetime, are the principal sources for K.32, K.34, K.40 and K.42 which are not in either the Venice or Parma manuscripts. The two Roseingrave volumes, containing the *Essercizi* and other compositions besides those just mentioned, were published in London in 1738-39 and again, from the same engraved plates with minor corrections, in 1754-56 (ca.) and in 1790.

The two Boivin volumes duplicate the contents of the Roseingrave edition but the works are in a different order. The statement on the title page of Volume I that the contents had never before been engraved appears to be incorrect. Although undated, it is believed that the Boivin edition was published in Paris in 1742, several years after the first Roseingrave edition.

There are some small differences between the Boivin and Roseingrave editions, chiefly in ornamentation and slurs. These are detailed in the footnotes of the pieces in which they occur in the new engraving of the present volume.

THE AVISON VERSION

The English organist-composer Charles Avison transcribed some of the Scarlatti sonatas for small string orchestra, using the *concerto grosso* form. Twelve of these were published at Newcastle upon Tyne in 1744. Avison's source was probably the Roseingrave edition. The present volume contains three sonatas which he used as the basis for his transcriptions: K.89b, first movement, Concerto III (page 30); K.88d, third movement, Concerto VII (page 28); K.81d, third movement, Concerto VIII (page 20). A comparison of the facsimile below with the new engraving on page 20 illustrates the freedom Avison exercised throughout the transcriptions. Measures are added and deleted, rhythmic figures, ornamentations and phrasings are changed and even time signatures and tempo indications are altered on occasion. Changes like these illustrate the versatility of themes in early music and how well they can be adapted not only to different instrumentations but also to entirely different moods. The facsimile also shows the early tradition in writing slurs to indicate notes played with a single bow stroke and vertical dashes to indicate notes played with separate strokes. *Tutti* means that all the instruments in the ensemble play together; *soli,* that only a smaller group play. All of this information, stemming from one of Scarlatti's contemporaries, is of great importance and has been taken into consideration in the editing of the present volume.

Facsimile of the Violino Concertino part of Avison's Concerto VIII.
The third movement is based on Sonata K.81, fourth movement.
Courtesy of the Trustees of the British Museum.

THE LONGO EDITION

Alessandro Longo's astounding edition, *Opere Complete per Clavicembalo de Domenico Scarlatti* (Milan, 1906), is one of the truly remarkable publications of the early twentieth century. He arranged contrasting sonatas into *Suites* based on tonal organization, assigning to each a catalog number which was the standard reference for many years. The following observations are made so that the performer may have a basis upon which to evaluate the use of Longo's edition today.

Modern research has made available extensive authentic information about early 18th-century performance practices of which Longo was seemingly unaware. In general his presentation of notes and rhythm is accurate; however, all of the phrasing slurs, staccatos, dynamics, and pedalling reflect his own concepts which are based on the romantic, pianistic style that followed Scarlatti's time at a distance of 80-100 years. Scarlatti's harmonic progressions are so unusual, in many cases, that Longo seems to have been unable to accept them as being correct, and in numerous instances dissonant notes have been removed from chords. These changes are sometimes, but not always, footnoted and as a result, many passages which are excitingly dissonant in their original form are rendered blandly consonant.

Longo seems not to have known that *tr* and ᴧᴧ were used interchangeably to indicate the trill, and that the standard baroque trill invariably began on the upper auxiliary (see the discussion of Trills on page 7). As a result, his fingering always indicates trills that begin on their main note and he frequently enforces this interpretation by adding an appoggiatura before the trill, on the main note. These procedures cause the trill to sound like the so-called "inverted mordent," an ornament beginning on the main note which is not known to have been used by Scarlatti or his contemporaries.

Many subsequent editions have been based on Longo's text, but because it is not always possible to identify his interpolations and deletions, they also perpetuate some of Longo's errors. It has seemed unnecessary to reiterate these errors in the footnotes of the new engraving on pages 14-63; therefore, only particularly significant alterations have been mentioned.

EXPLANATION OF THE K. AND L. NUMBERS

For many years, Alessandro Longo's complete edition of the Scarlatti sonatas was the only available collection which made any attempt at organization. Longo arbitrarily grouped them into *Suites* without regard for apparent chronology of the manuscript sources, assigning a number to each of them for reference. Since that time, Ralph Kirkpatrick, in his definitive study *Domenico Scarlatti* (Princeton, 1953) has recatalogued all of the sonatas in the apparent chronological order, and his numbers seem destined to replace the older ones of Longo. For the convenience of performers who are famliar with only one system, both the K. (Kirkpatrick) and L. (Longo) numbers are given.

STYLE AND FORM OF SCARLATTI'S SONATAS

Late in the baroque era musical style began to change, gradually developing into the early classic style of Mozart and Haydn. This transitional period was called *galant*. Scarlatti was born in 1685, the same year as J.S. Bach and Handel who composed mainly in the baroque style, but his music, as Robert Donington remarks in *The Interpretation of Early Music* (London, 1963), is entirely galant. Elegance and light-heartedness characterize galant style. Phrases often had odd numbers of measures, and voices were added and deleted freely in the polyphonic texture. The form of composition became less rigid in galant style and the short theme with its almost infinite variations, a characteristic of the baroque style, began to be more extended and developed. Unprepared dissonance became acceptable and many of Scarlatti's harmonic progressions which sound original and pleasingly dissonant to modern ears shocked some of his contemporaries. His musical innovations aroused much comment. Dr. Charles Burney, the celebrated English music historian and critic, was well acquainted with C.P.E. Bach, Thomas Roseingrave and many other of Scarlatti's contemporaries. He made the following remark about the new style of music in *The Present State of Music in Germany* (1775):

"There are several traits in the characters of the younger Scarlatti and Emmanuel Bach, which bear a strong resemblance. Both were sons of great and popular composers, regarded as standards of perfection by all their contemporaries, except their own children, who dared to explore new ways to fame. Domenico Scarlatti, half a century ago, hazarded notes of taste and effect, at which other musicians have but just arrived, and to which the public ear is but lately reconciled; Emmanuel Bach, in like manner, seems to have outstript his age."

In the same book, Burney relates the following about M. L'Augier, an intimate friend of Scarlatti:

"Scarlatti frequently told M. L'Augier that he was sensible he had broke through all the rules of composition in his lessons; but asked if his deviations from these rules offended the ear? and, upon being answered in the negative, he said, that he thought there was scarce any other rule, worth the attention of a man of genius, than that of not displeasing the only sense of which music is the object."

Although the great majority of Scarlatti's sonatas are in binary form with each half repeated, there are some multi-movement works having sections in contrasting tempos. Some individual movements, which are well able to stand by themselves, are included in the present volume and may be identified by the letter beside the K. number. (See the discussion on page 5). The only composition included that is not in binary form is K. 89b, an expressive slow movement.

SCARLATTI'S DA CAPO INDICATIONS

Da capo, or its abbreviation *D.C.* appears at the end of some of the sonatas, and has usually been omitted in other editions. The procedure of repeating binary repeated movements over again from the beginning does not seem too representative of the custom during Scarlatti's lifetime. However, since there appears to be no evidence that the term *da capo* was used with any other meaning, we cannot positively conclude that it was not done, or that Scarlatti himself did not intend the sonatas to be re-played where indicated. The performer will have to judge for himself how best to perform them.

INTERPRETATION

The instructions for performance style and ornamentation in the following pages may be found in C.P.E. Bach's famous *Essay on the True Art of Playing Keyboard Instruments* (Berlin, 1753). It is important to note that none of these instructions conflict with similar practices which had been well established throughout Europe for many years. The writings of Scarlatti's contemporaries, Tosi and Geminiani, and the important treatises by L. Mozart, *A Treatise on the Fundamental Principles of Violin Playing* (Augsburg, 1756) and J.J. Quantz, *On Playing the Flute* (Berlin, 1752), provide further corroboration of these practices. We may, therefore, be certain that they correspond to a style which Scarlatti would have considered correct. The editorial suggestions in light print in the new engraving on pages 14-63 are based on this information.

ORNAMENTATION

APPOGGIATURA: The appoggiatura, written in small print before its main note, is commonly called a *grace note* today. Appoggiatura derives from *appoggiare*, to lean, and is an accented dissonance played on the beat and taking its time value from the main note. A small breath, or silence of articulation, is made before the appoggiatura which is always slurred softly to the main note, whether a slur is written or not. Scarlatti's appoggiaturas are written as eighths, sixteenths or thirty-seconds, all of which have the same meaning. It is the value of the main note and its context that determine the length of the appoggiatura and not its notation.

LONG APPOGGIATURA: Most appoggiaturas are long and take half the time value of their main note.

Long appoggiaturas may take two-thirds of the value of a main note which is dotted.

SHORT APPOGGIATURA: The short appoggiatura is an incisive accent which takes very little time from its main note. It is frequently found before a quick rhythmic group.

SCHLEIFER OR SLIDE: This ornament is a two-note appoggiatura beginning a third above or below its main note. It begins on the beat and is played quickly and gracefully.

THE TRILL: Following the prevailing custom of the time, Scarlatti used ∿ and *tr* interchangeably to indicate the trill. The more familiar *tr* sign is used throughout the present volume. The trill begins on the upper auxiliary (the note above the written, or main, note) and alternates rapidly with the main note. Trills begin on the beat of the main note and must have at least four notes. For example, the

trill written: may be played: or:

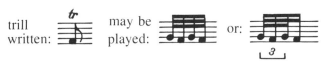

On quick notes there is usually not enough time for more than a four-note trill, but the performer may add more repercussions on a longer note to suit his taste and skill. The first note may be accented and prolonged slightly and a long trill may accelerate. The last note must be the main note and the trill may not slow down although it may come to rest at any time after the required four notes have been played.

This trill   may be played:

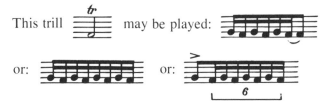

or: or:

TRILL WITH SUFFIX OR TERMINATION

Scarlatti sometimes wrote a termination in small notes after the trill. Regardless of their notated time value, these little notes are played at the same speed as the trill. The terminated trill requires a minimum of 6 notes. The performer may add a termination consisting of the lower auxiliary and main note to any trill that is followed by the next higher or lower scale note.

written: played:

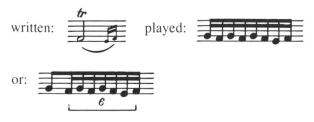

or:

Alternatively, a termination which anticipates the next note may be added to a trill. The trill comes to rest before its full time value and the following note is played very quickly in anticipation of the next main note.

written: played:

written: played:

A trill that is followed by a double bar, a rest or a main note which is further away than the next scale note should not have a termination added to it.

SUBSTITUTE FOR THE TRILL ON QUICK NOTES

An upper appoggiatura may be substituted for a trill on a quick note if the performer cannot play the required four notes. The appoggiatura will fulfill the dissonant function of the upper auxiliary beginning of the trill.

For example, this figure:

may be played:

OTHER ORNAMENTS: THE MORDENT AND THE TURN

Although Scarlatti's contemporaries used the mordent and turn signs extensively, both ornaments are fully written out wherever they appear in the Venice and Parma manuscripts. The ornament signs appear in the Roseingrave edition, however, in K.34 and K.42, neither of which is in the manuscripts. (A further discussion of these sources will be found on page 4.)

MORDENT. The mordent (from *mordere*, to bite) is an incisive accent. It begins on the beat, on the main note, moves quickly and lightly to the lower auxiliary and returns at once to the main note, remaining there until the entire time value is completed. On a longer note, there may be more repercussions.

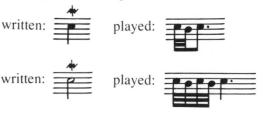

TURN. A comparison of J.S. Bach's Table of Ornaments in the *Clavier-Büchlein vor Wilhelm Friedemann Bach,* shows that the turn sign placed diagonally above a note is identical with the horizontally placed turn described by C.P.E. Bach and other early writers. Many editors mistake this sign for a terminated trill, however, its proper interpretation consists of the upper auxiliary, main note, lower auxiliary and main note. When placed over a note, the turn begins on the beat and is spread evenly to fill the entire time value of the main note.

RHYTHMIC ALTERATIONS

THE VARIABLE DOT

The dot beside a note in baroque music had a variable length. C.P.E. Bach says "the short notes which follow dotted notes are always shorter in execution than their notated length." This point is of such importance that all the early writers emphasize it repeatedly. The custom, often called "overdotting," is used in such places as K.89b, measure 15, where the figure written:

ACCOMMODATED RHYTHMS

In compositions where the triplet rhythm predominates, measures notated in ordinary eighths should be accommodated to the triplet figure by lengthening the first of two notes and shortening the second, in the following manner:

K.391, measures 34 and 35

written:

should be played:

In measure 36, the rhythm is overdotted to correspond to the triplet figure.

written: played:

PHRASING, ARTICULATION AND FINGERING

One of the dominant features of early music is the use of short themes reiterated throughout the composition in many variants. The unity of style which this produces is best exemplified by selecting a particular phrasing and articulation for each short motive, or little thematic grouping of notes, and preserving it throughout the composition. A further aid in projecting style is based on the early concept that fingering and phrasing are one and the same. The fingering in light print in the present volume utilizes this concept. Whenever practical, the short motive has identical fingering in all of its appearances and the shift of the hand across the keyboard is made to coincide with silences of articulation. Context, and the awkwardness which sometimes results when using the thumb or fifth finger on black keys, sometimes affect the choice of fingering. The performer should feel free to change fingerings which are unsuitable to his hand, but uniformity of phrase groupings should be the important factor in selecting different fingering.

There is a great wealth of original slur signs in Scarlatti's music, compared with other manuscripts of the same era. Often, only a few are used to establish a pattern which is to be continued. Slurs over notes which form a broken chord indicate notes to be collected and held under the hand until the chord is complete. The slurs added in light print follow these principles and other prevailing performance customs of the time. Stepwise successions tend to be legato and wide skips and passages with many skips tend to be more articulate. "Ordinary movement," described by the early writers as appropriate to most *allegros*, consists of slightly detaching all the notes in proportion to their time value. This enhances the briskness of the *allegro* by imparting sparkle and clarity. Slower movements are played much more seriously and with many sustained notes.

The silences of articulation or small "breaths" which divide phrases into intelligible groups are a most important consideration in early music. Articulations are required before all appoggiaturas (see also the discussion under ORNAMENTATION and are customary before syncopations, wide skips, long tied notes, and frequently before a change in prevailing note values in a passage. Detachments indicated by staccato dots in the present volume should not be played abruptly. The notes should be held for approximately half their time value.

DYNAMICS

The gradual increases and decreases in volume which are possible on the piano are extremely limited on the harpsichord, for which these compositions were written. Most of the dynamic effects, as a result, are built into the music by such devices as contrast of high and low registers, use of many dissonances which were conventionally accented, suspended harmonies which were played louder than their resolutions, expanding sequences which build up tension and volume, and echo effects. Rapidly moving notes are juxtaposed against slower ones, voices are added and deleted freely to thicken and thin the texture, rests are used expressively. All these effects are readily transferable to the piano and eliminate the need for excesses in swell shadings. The dynamics suggested in light print are based on the foregoing principles. The performer, however, must judge for himself whether to use them or to select his own.

The dynamics in the Avison version have been considered for the first time in this volume. Avison states in his *Essay on Musical Expression* (London, 1752) that "to do a composition justice, it must be played in a taste and style exactly corresponding to the intention of the composer as to preserve and illustrate all the beauties of the work." See also the discussion of the Avison version on page 4.

PEDAL

The harpsichord has no equivalent to the damper pedal on the piano. While it may, perhaps, be used occasionally for accent, it should never bind together notes which cannot be held down by the fingers. It is recommended that the pianist learn these sparkling works without any damper pedal and judge for himself whether the clarity of the structure does not stand well by itself without the addition of a tone color which was unknown during Scarlatti's lifetime.

FIGURED BASS

A few of Scarlatti's sonatas have figured basses, a form of writing typical of the period. Those included in the present volume are K.73c, K.80, K.81d, K.88c, K.88d and K.89b. The figures and accidentals in dark print below the bass staff indicate the harmony which is represented by the written melody and bass. The performer may fill up the sound by adding the notes called for by the figures, adjusting the fullness of the chords to suit the context of each particular passage.

Figured bass is derived from triadic harmony in common use in the 17th and 18th centuries and is subject to the rules of voice leading, doubling, etc., which governed it. In a fully figured bass, each bass note is accounted for by either the presence or absence of figures. However, Scarlatti only partially figured these basses in places where the correct harmony might be ambiguous or not immediately apparent to the performer.

Although a detailed study of figured bass is necessary to understand this practice fully, the performer who knows triads and inversions may fill in some of the harmonies. Notes may be added in either treble or bass, but they may not be higher than the soprano nor lower than the bass notes written by the composer. The following brief explanation will illustrate simple ways in which the figures in these sonatas may be used. 5 indicates that the 5th of the chord must be the highest note, that is, in the soprano.

An accidental by itself alters the 3rd above the written bass. (Sometimes the 3 is written also, but more often it is not.)

K.89b, measure 15
written: may be played:

K.88c, measure 17,
written: may be played:

 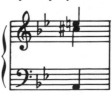

An accidental beside another number tells what interval is to be altered above the written bass note.

K.89b, measure 7,

written:

may be played:

Usually, a number by itself tells what inversion of the triad is being used. 6 stands for a first inversion. The notes to be filled in are the 6th and 3rd above the bass. Because the sonatas are written in two voices, the missing note may be supplied between the written ones.

K.73c, measure 2,
written: may be played:

$\frac{6}{4}$ indicates a triad in second inversion. The notes which may be filled in are the 6th and 4th above the bass.

K.88c, measure 43,
written: may be played: or:

7 stands for a seventh chord in root position. The notes which may be filled in are the 7th, 5th and 3rd above the bass.

K.88c, measure 25,
written: may be played:

$\frac{6}{5}$ stands for a seventh chord in first inversion. The notes which may be added are the 6th, 5th and 3rd above the bass.

K.88c, measure 27,
written: may be played:

6, 76, 98, 43 show that one of the upper voices is changing from the first to the second interval above the same bass note.

K.88d, measure 2,
written: may be played:

K.80, measure 9
written: may be played:

Where two separate signs are given, each has its own interpretation. In measure 31 of K.88d, the flat above the staff alters the 3rd above the bass. The 6 below the staff indicates a triad in first inversion.

K.88d, measure 31
written: may be played: or:

The harmonic texture of these sonatas should not be overloaded and only those notes which contribute to the beauty of the passage should be added.

ACKNOWLEDGMENTS

I would like to thank the directors of the Biblioteca Nationale Marciana, Venice, for their kind permission to reproduce facsimiles from the manuscript copies of the Scarlatti sonatas and the Library of Congress, Washington, D.C. for kind permission to reproduce a portion of the Avison Concertos. I would also like to acknowledge with thanks the kind use of microfilms of early 18th century editions for study and comparison which were made available by the King's College, Cambridge, the British Museum and the Library of Congress. I especially wish to thank Willard A. Palmer for his invaluable advice and suggestions in the preparation of the present volume and Judith Simon Linder for her valued assistance in the preparation of the manuscript. In particular I wish to thank Iris and Morton Manus for the meticulous care with which they have helped me to prepare this edition.

Facsimile of Minuet K.440, L.97 from the Venice Manuscripts
Courtesy of the Biblioteca Nationale Marciana, Venice

Measure numbers have been added for study purposes

This Minuet appears on pages 56-59.

EARLY TRADITIONS IN MUSIC WRITING

There are some early traditions in music writing which should be explained to make it possible for the student to use the facsimile of the Venice manuscript.

KEY SIGNATURES

The key signature is only one flat (Bb) although the Minuet is in the key of B-flat major. Key signatures evolved during the late 16th and 17th centuries as the use of transposed modes became more common. It was not until later, however, that the notation of key signatures reflected the change of tonality from the modes to the present major or minor, resulting in much music which appears to have one less flat or sharp in the key signature than it should. The missing one, however, is always written as an accidental wherever it occurs. Since only the appearance of the page is changed, we have altered the key signatures throughout the present volume, removed redundant accidentals, and supplied necessary natural signs to conform to modern notation.

ACCIDENTALS

Unless altered notes were consecutive, a separate accidental was required for each, regardless of the number of times it occured in the same measure. The bar line did not have the function of cancelling an accidental. For example, the flat before E in measure 43 of K.440 remains effective for the next note even though it is in the next measure. In measures 17 and 21, which are duplicates, the absence of a flat on the last E is very probably an error. As written, the measure would be played:

A similar problem occurs in duplicate measures 41 and 45. The ear may possibly accept the progression with E-natural in measures 17 and 21, but in measures 17

and 21 it simply sounds incorrect. Many times, errors in early music are readily correctable; however, the same errors appear in the Parma copy of this Minuet also. In cases of this type, the performer must decide for himself which progression he prefers.

DIRECTS

The sign at the end of the line containing measures 31-38, is called a direct. Its purpose in the blank staff after the bar line is to show the pitch of the first note on the next line of music.

SLURS

The indefiniteness of some slurs can be noticed in measure 17 and other places. The custom of indicating only a few slurs in figures which are repeated is clearly shown in this Minuet. Because the performer was expected to play all similar groups with similar phrasing, the slurs in measures 3, 9 and 10, for example, are effective for measures 1, 2, 4, 11, 12 and 13 as well.

FIRST AND SECOND ENDINGS

The slurs in measure 56, together with the little hand and Spanish directions, comprise an indication for first and second endings. The words instruct the performer to omit measure 56 when playing the repeat and to use the last 4 measures for the conclusion. The modern form of writing first and second endings is used in the new engraving on page 59.

Fermate at double bars in early music are decorative or simply indicate the conclusion of the composition. They have been omitted in the new engraving.

ARIA

K, 32; L, 423

(a) All of the trills in this *Aria* may be played with more repercussions or without terminations. See the discussion on page 7.

MINUETTO

K.73b; L.217

(a) This is the second of three movements which comprise **K.73**.

(b) It is impossible to determine where some of the slurs in the Venice manuscript begin and end. The very clear ones have provided sufficient information to draw the remaining ones in conformity with customary performance practices. See the discussion of PHRASING AND ARTICULATION on page 9.

(c) See the discussion on page 7 for other styles in which the trills may be played in this *Minuetto*.

d   The *piano* indication is one of the very few dynamic markings in the original manuscripts.

e   The *Minuetto* on the next two pages is the last movement of K.73. *Segue* is a direction to the performer to begin without pausing between movements. Although each *Minuet* may be played separately, the performer may wish to play them as a pair.

MINUETTO

K.73c; L.217

Allegro M.M. ♪ = 116-120

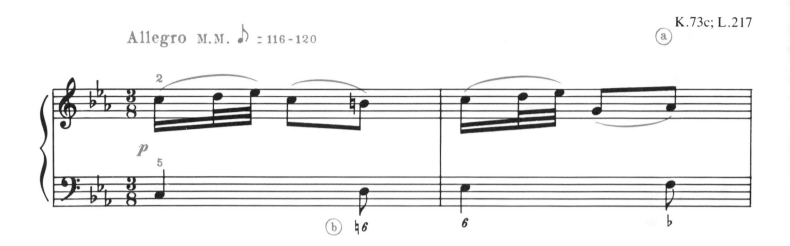

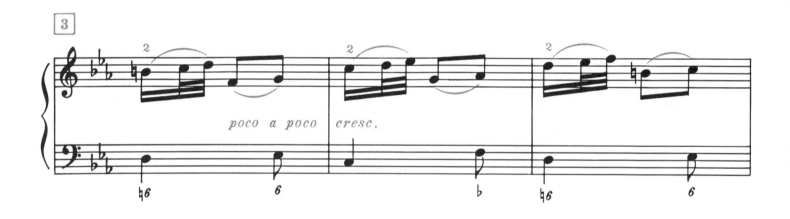

poco a poco cresc.

ⓐ This *Minuetto* and the preceding one on pages 16-17 are the concluding movements of K.73. Although it may be performed separately, the Venice manuscript, marked *segue,* indicates that it is to be begun immediately after K.73b.

ⓑ The numbers and accidentals in dark print are figured basses. They are explained on pages 10 and 11.

ⓒ The trills may be played with more repercussions. See the discussion on page 7.

ⓓ The *Da Capo* in Scarlatti's music is discussed on page 6.

SONATA

K.81d; L.271

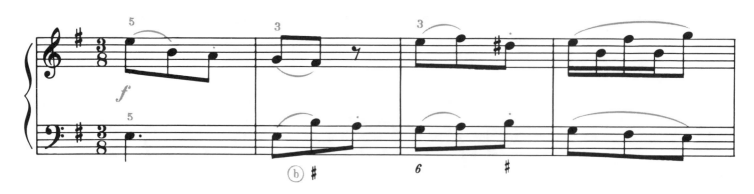

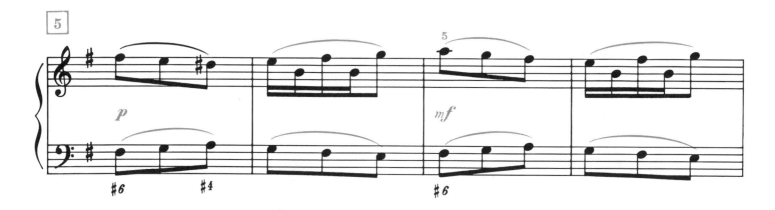

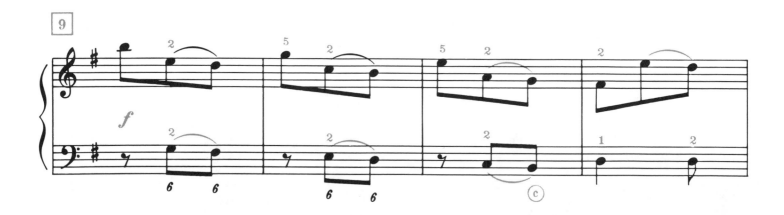

The placement of some of the slurs in the Venice manuscript is so indefinite that it is impossible to tell exactly where they begin and end. We have drawn them in conformity with the style of those which are very clear, perpetuating the style throughout.

(a) This is the last of four movements which comprise K.81. Avison used it as the basis for the third movement of *Concerto VIII*. He changed the time signature to ¾ and the tempo to *Amoroso*. The dynamics in light print are suggested by the Avison version. Further discussion and a facsimile from the Avison version will be found on page 4.

(b) The numbers and accidentals in dark print are figured basses. They are explained on pages 10 and 11.

(c) The B is misprinted as A in the Venice manuscript. The measure corresponds to measures 18, 41 and 47.

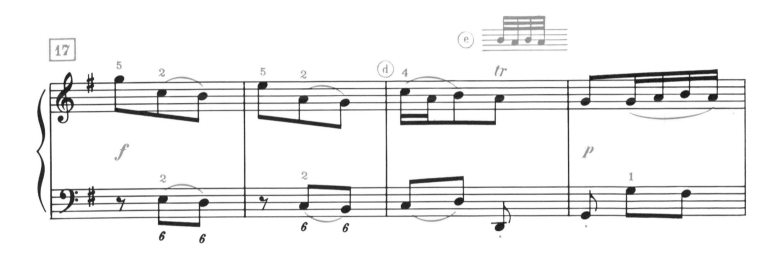

ⓓ The Longo edition and those copied from his text have the rhythm in this measure printed incorrectly as follows:

ⓔ See the discussion on page 7 for other styles in which the trills in this Sonata may be played.

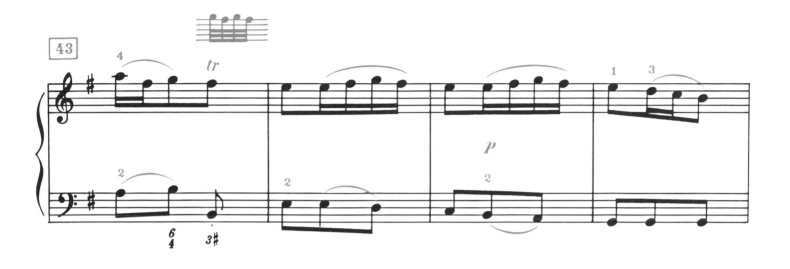

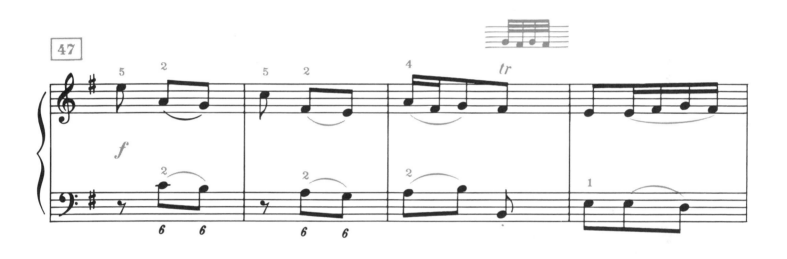

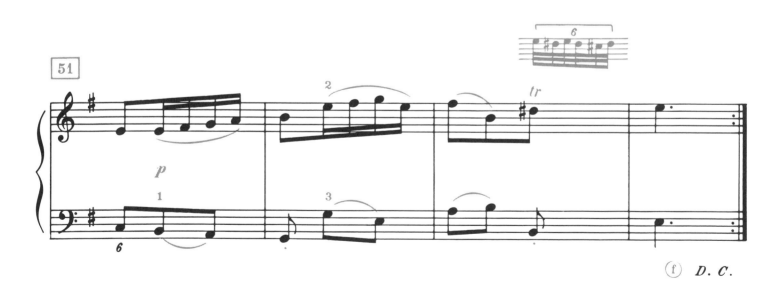

(f) *D. C.*

(f) A discussion of the *D.C.* here and in several other sonatas will be found on page 6.

SONATA

Allegro M.M. ♩ = 96-112

This is the shortest of all the Scarlatti sonatas discovered to date.

(a) This D is missing in the Parma manuscript.

(b) The rhythm of the eighths in this measure should be altered to accommodate to the prevailing triplets. ACCOMMODATED RHYTHM is explained on page 8. The trill may have more repercussions. See the discussion on page 7.

SONATA

Allegro M.M. ♩ = 96-108

K.88c; L.36

ⓐ   This is the third of four movements which comprise K.88.

ⓑ   Instead of a short appoggiatura here and in measure 20, the performer may prefer a long one, as follows: See the discussion on pages 6 and 7.

ⓒ   The numbers and accidentals in dark print are figured basses. They are explained on pages 10 and 11.

ⓓ   Other styles in which the trills in this Sonata may be played are discussed on page 7.

(e) In Longo and editions copied from his text, G is an eighth note instead of a quarter.

27

MINUET

K.88d; L.36

(a) This is the last of four movements in K.88. It was used by Avison as the basis for the third movement of *Concerto VII*. In addition to many other changes, the time signature was changed to ¾; instead of being a *Minuet*, it is an *Adagio* in Avison's version. A facsimile from the Avison *Concertos* and a further discussion will be found on page 4.

(b) The numbers and accidentals in dark print are figured basses. They are explained on pages 10 and 11.

(c) The trills may be played without termination, or with more repercussions. See the discussion on page 7.

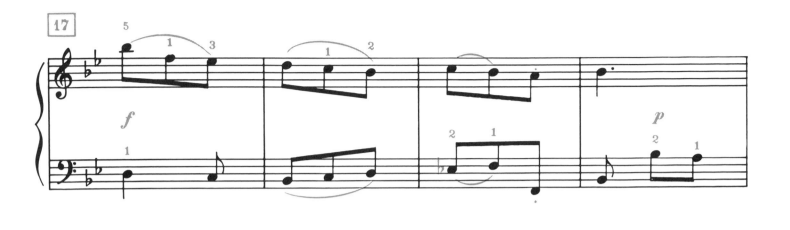

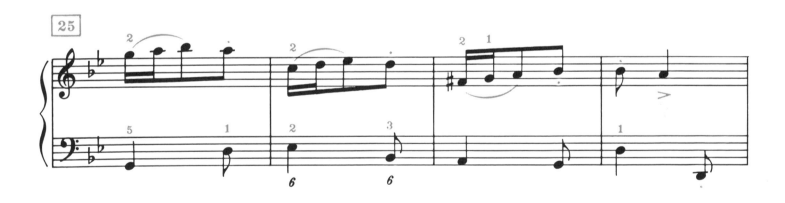

SONATA

K.89b; L.211

Ⓐ

Grave M.M. ♩ = 60 - 66

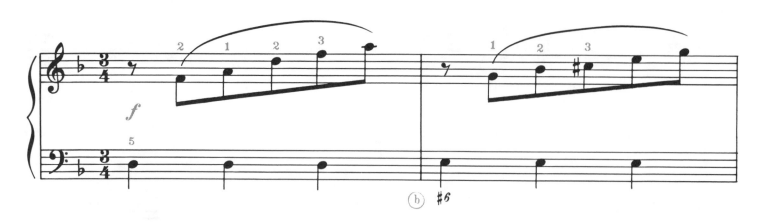

Ⓐ This is the second of three movements in **K.89**. Avison used it for the first movement of his *Concerto III*. A facsimile and discussion of the Avison version will be found on page 4. The dynamics in light print are suggested by this version.

Ⓑ The numbers and accidentals in dark print are figured basses. They are explained on pages 10 and 11.

Ⓒ This trill may be simplified and played without termination. See the discussion on page 7.

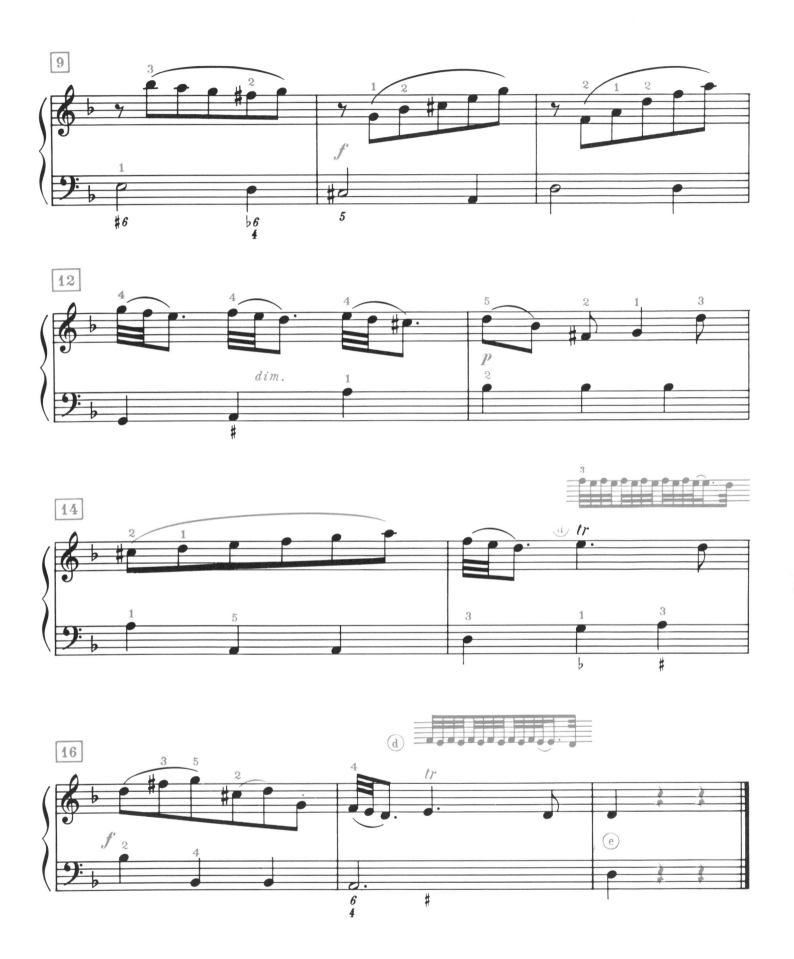

ⓓ The baroque custom of lengthening the dot beside a note and shortening the following note is illustrated in the light print realization of this trill and the one in measure 17. The trills may be played with fewer repercussions. See the discussion on pages 7 and 8.

ⓔ The Longo edition and those prepared from his text have dotted half notes in this measure instead of quarter notes. A discussion of these editions will be found on page 5.

MINUET

K.77b; L.168

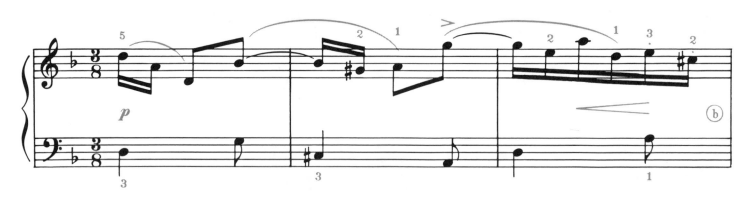

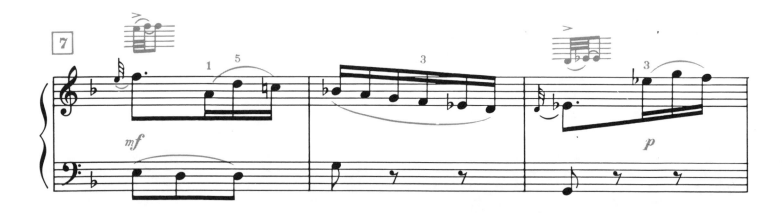

(a) This is the second of two movements which comprise K.77.

(b) Longo has inserted the following measure between measures 3 and 4. It is not in the Venice manuscript. A further discussion of changes Longo made in his edition will be found on page 5.

(c) All of the appoggiaturas in this *Minuet* have been realized as short appoggiaturas; however, the performer may play them as long appoggiaturas if he prefers. For example, measure 5 may be played: The same interpretation should be used for all the appoggiaturas whether short or long. For a further discussion, see pages 6 and 7.

poco a poco cresc.

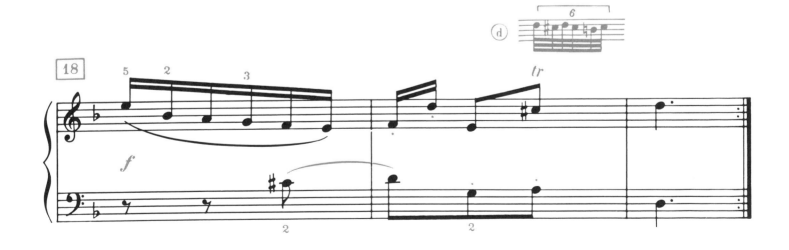

ⓓ   Different styles in which this trill and the trill in measure 39 may be played are discussed on page 7.

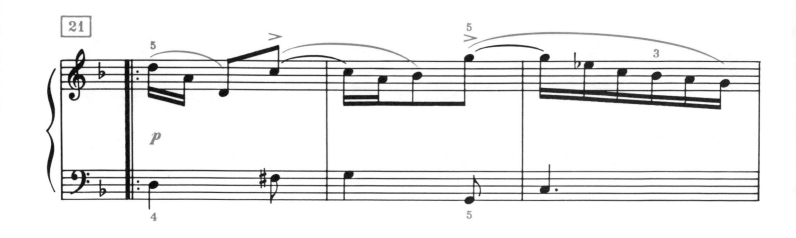

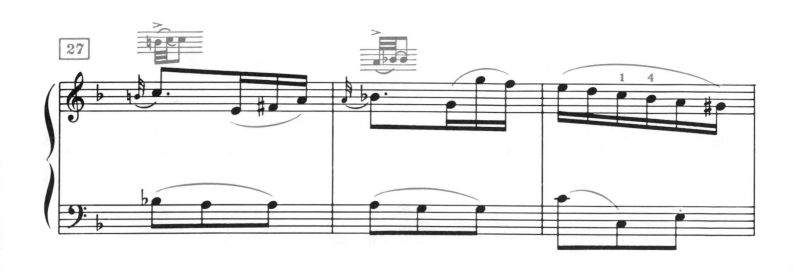

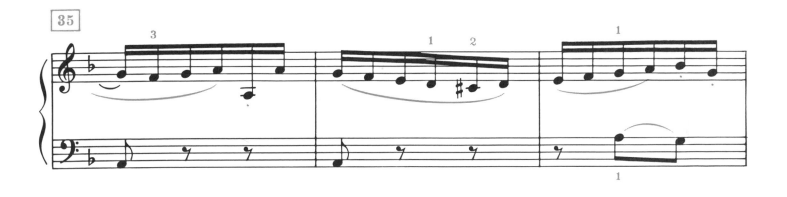

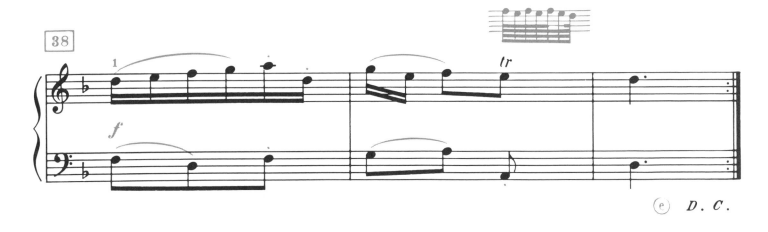

ⓔ   A discussion of the *D.C.* which appears in several Scarlatti sonatas will be found on page 6.

MINUET

K.83b; L.S.31

(a) This is the second of two movements which comprise K.83.

ⓑ See page 7 for a discussion of other styles in which the trills may be played.

SONATA

K.34; L.S.7

There are small engraving differences between the Roseingrave and Boivin editions. Dots beside the half notes in measures 12 and 28, dots beside the double bars, and the slurs in measures 21, 25 and 26 are clear in the Boivin edition but missing in Roseingrave. These editions are discussed further on page 3.

(a) The A is missing in some modern editions.

(b) In the Longo edition and those copied from it, this E has been changed to F.

(c)   In the Longo edition and those copied from it, this C has been changed to B-flat.

(d)   Although the required sharp beside this F is missing in Roseingrave and Boivin editions, it is undoubtedly an engraver's error. See the discussion of EARLY TRADITIONS IN MUSIC WRITING on page 13.

MINUET

K.80; not in Longo
ⓐ

ⓐ This *Minuet*, the second of two movements in K. 79, is missing from the Longo edition. The Kirkpatrick catalog provides it with a separate number, K.80, for positive identification. A discussion of the K. and L. numbers and of the Longo edition is on page 5.

ⓑ The numbers and accidentals in dark print are figured basses. They are explained on pages 10 and 11.

ⓒ In accordance with early traditions in music writing, there should be a sharp written before this F; however, it is missing in the Venice manuscript. A further explanation will be found on page 13.

ⓓ For a discussion of other styles in which the trills may be played, see page 7.

ⓔ The *Da Capo* indication in Scarlatti's work is discussed on page 6.

SONATA

K.90d; L.106

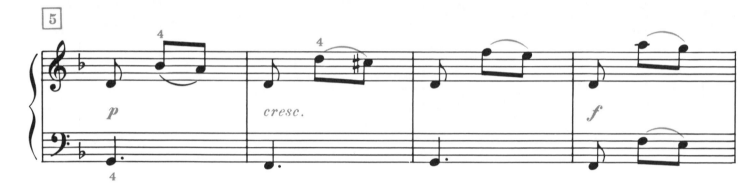

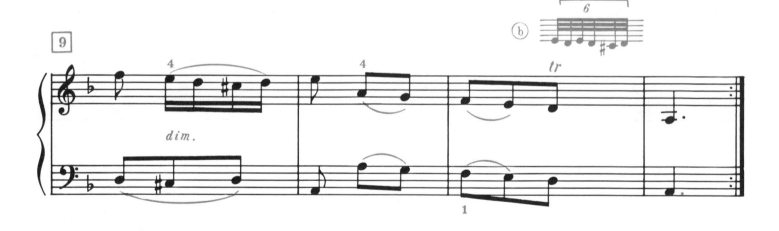

ⓐ   This is the fourth movement of K.90.

ⓑ   Other styles in which the trills may be played are discussed on page 7.

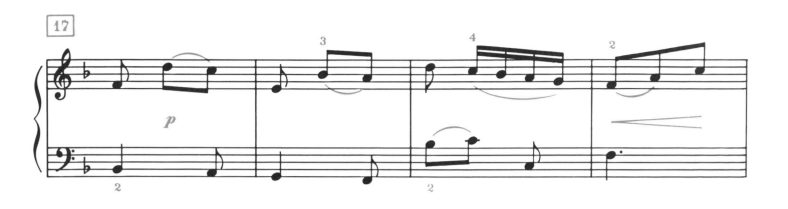

ⓒ   A discussion of the *Da Capo* in Scarlatti's works will be found on page 6.

MINUETTO

Allegro M.M. ♩ = 120-126

K.42; L.S.36

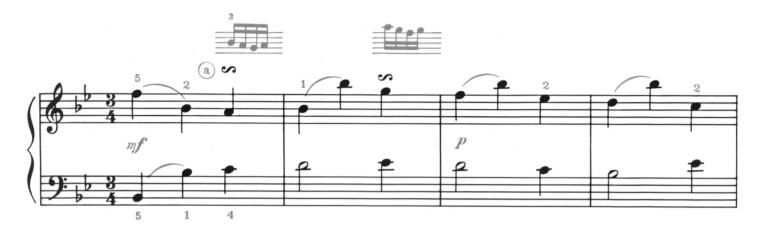

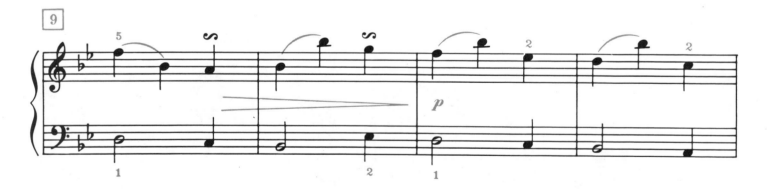

(a) This *Minuetto*, not found in either the Venice or Parma manuscripts, is in the Roseingrave and Boivin editions described on page 3. None of the turns are in the Boivin edition although they are in both Roseingrave editions, apparently added by Roseingrave himself. The performer may decide for himself whether to play them or not. The trills are in all editions. A further discussion of the turn will be found on page 8.

(b) The trills may have more repercussions or terminations. See the discussion on page 7.

ⓒ The Roseingrave and Boivin editions use this symbol ⌁ to indicate the terminated trill in this measure. Because Scarlatti is not known to have used this symbol himself, it has been indicated here with the conventional ***tr***

MINUETTO

Allegro M.M. ♩ = 120 – 138

K.40; L.357

(a)　See the discussion on page 7 for other styles in which this trill and those in measures 11 and 23 may be played.

PASTORAL

Allegro M.M. ♩. = 96-116

K.415; L.S.11

ⓐ The trills may be played with more repercussions. See the discussion on page 7.

(b) This measure is a duplicate of measure 27. The F♯ is incorrectly printed as a D in the Venice manuscript. It is F♯ in both places in the Parma manuscript. Longo and the editions made from his text have the incorrect D in this measure.

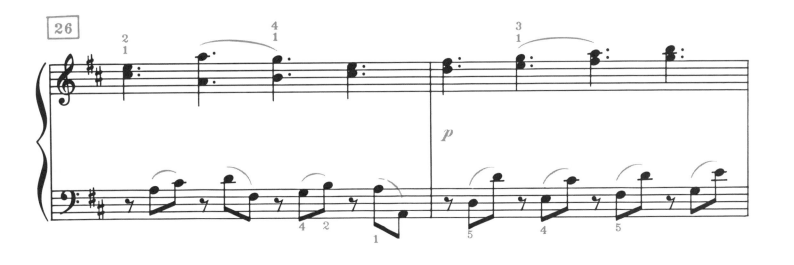

MINUET

The title *Minuet* is written in the Parma but not the Venice manuscript.

The trills may be played as simple, four-note trills without termination. See the discussion on page 7.

The slur for the appoggiatura is in the Venice but not the Parma manuscript.

ⓓ In both the Venice and Parma manuscripts, *Tacet* is written in these places to indicate that the lack of notes for the left hand is not an omission, but intended by the composer. Whole rests, used today for this purpose, have been added in light print. Some other EARLY TRADITIONS IN MUSIC WRITING are discussed on page 13.

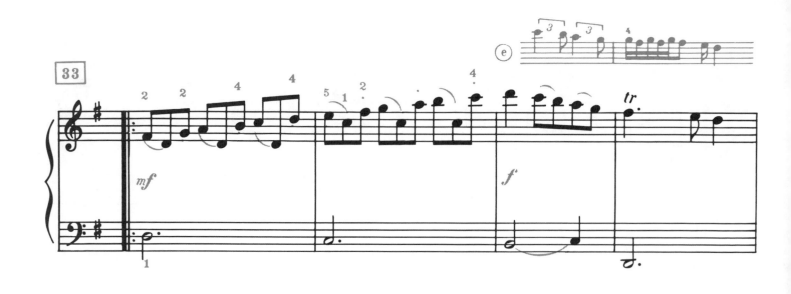

ⓔ   The realization of these two measures (in light print) illustrates two conventional alterations of rhythm which were practiced in this period: overdotting and accommodation. These are discussed on page 8.

MINUET

Allegro M.M. ♩ = 104 - 112

K.440; L.97

A facsimile of this *Minuet* as it appears in the Venice manuscript and a discussion of EARLY TRADITIONS IN MUSIC WRITING are on pages 12 and 13

ⓐ   The trills in this *Minuet* may be simplified in accordance with the instructions on page 7.

ⓑ Perhaps this E should be flat. See the discussion of ACCIDENTALS on page 13.

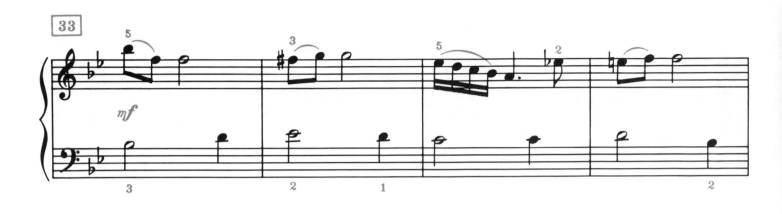

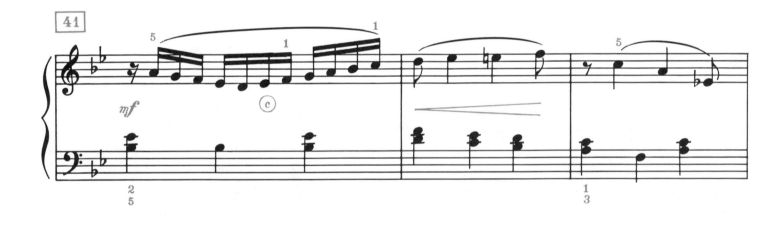

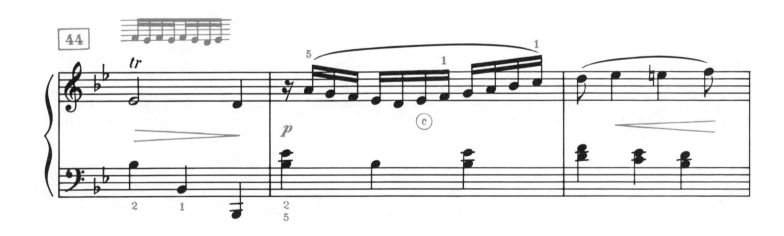

ⓒ Perhaps this E should be natural. See the discussion of ACCIDENTALS on page 13.

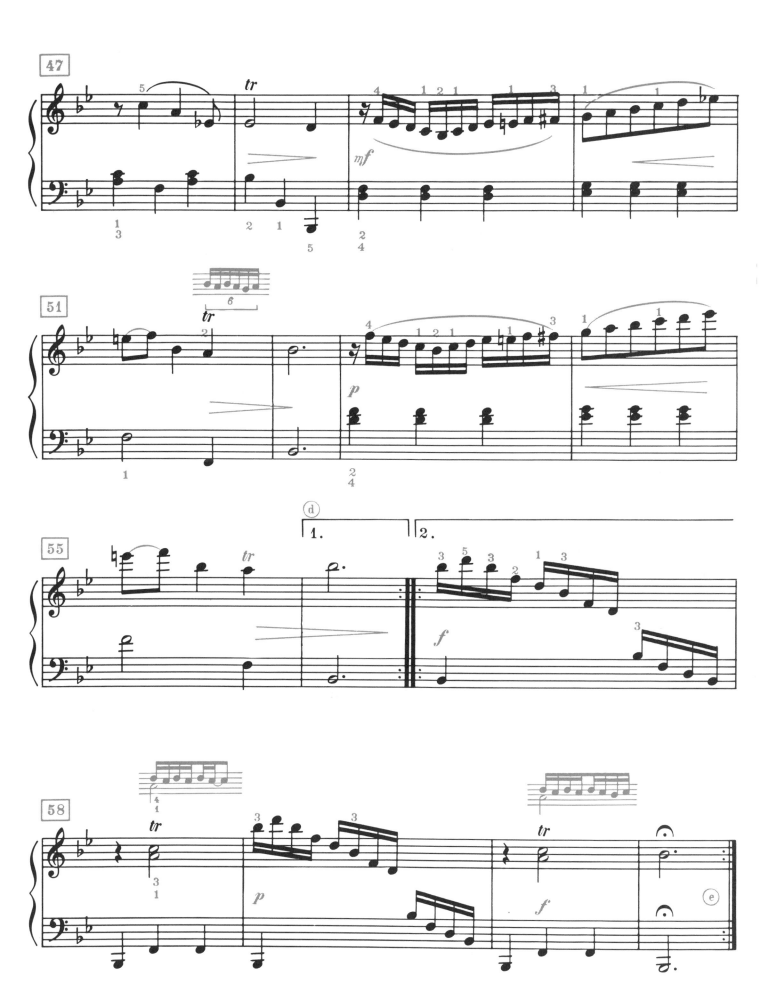

(d) An early tradition for indicating the first and second endings has been modernized in these measures. See the discussion and the facsimile on pages 12 and 13.

(e) These dots are in the Venice but not the Parma manuscript.

CAPRICCIO

K.63; L.84

ⓐ See the discussion on page 7 for other styles in which the trills may be played.

ⓑ According to prevailing tradition, the slurs in measures 20-23 and 48-51 indicate notes to be played and held throughout the measure because they form broken chords. A further discussion of slurs is on page 9.

Measure 20 should be performed as follows:

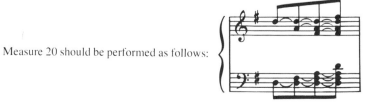

The other measures should follow the same style.

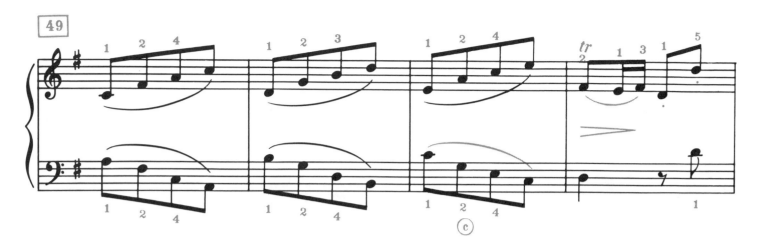

Engraved by Victor J. Mitchell

ⓒ   In the Longo edition and some of those copied from his text, this G has been changed to an A. A further discussion of the Longo edition is on page 5.

ⓓ   The natural sign has been changed to a flat in the Longo and other editions.

ⓔ   The tie between G's is missing in Longo and other editions. The flat before the B produces an unusual harmonic progression, but is very clear in the Venice manuscript. Other editions do not have the flat.

ⓕ   The *Da Capo* indication in Scarlatti's compositions is discussed on page 6.

THEMATIC INDEX